The World Turned Upside Down

1647 English Cartoon – 'The World Turned Upside Down'

The World Turned Upside Down

Geoffrey M. Hodgson

Illustrated by Jessie Agnew

Martlet Books

First published 2013 by

Martlet Books
8 Withers Close, Oakham
Rutland LE15 6GG
United Kingdom

www.martlet-books.co.uk

ISBN 978-0-9521853-6-9. Hardcover.

This volume is printed in a limited first edition of 300 copies.

This is copy number   241

Printed in the UK by CPI Group (UK), Croydon CR0 4YY.

For Amelia, Ewan, Oscar and Rhys

The World Turned Upside Down

Geoffrey M. Hodgson
Illustrated by Jessie Agnew

Contents

Listen to me and you shall hear,
    news hath not been this thousand year:

Since Herod, Caesar, and many more,
    you never heard the like before.
    …

Why should we from good Laws be bound?

Yet let's be content, and the times lament,
    you see the world turn'd upside down.

From the 1643 English Ballad,
The World Turned Upside Down

Preface

I have written a lot, but never before a children's story. The possibility of making the inversion of the social hierarchy into a tale for young people occurred to me as early as 1977. But I never pursued it further. When my daughter and son were born in the 1980s I was too busy with full-time work. Then, between October 2008 and February 2012, my wife and I were blessed with four delightful grandchildren. And by then I was working on a part-time contract.

The final push was a conversation in Jinan with one of my Chinese students (Zhang Xueqi) on the multi-faceted and satirical potential of this youthful genre. I finished the first complete draft in two long days in China in 2012. I warmly thank my family for critical reactions and helpful suggestions for improvement, although stubbornly I have not followed them all. I am also particularly grateful to Jessie Agnew – the mother of two of my grandchildren – for her charming illustrations.

Finally I thank Hannah Dore (aged 8), Rebecca Dore (aged 10) William Dore (aged 10), and Thomas Dore (aged 13) for listening to the first reading of the book and providing valuable feedback in the final stages.

Geoffrey M. Hodgson

October 2013

1. The Country with No Name

A long time ago, there was a small country that no-one put on a map, and no-one knew its name. This country was neither rich nor poor. Its people were mostly but not extremely happy, and nothing much happened to make them sad. Day after day, week after week, month after month, and year after year, they carried on with their ordinary lives.

In this country with no name, everyone had a job to do, and everyone knew their place. There was a royal family, and its ruler was King Boris. He was married to Queen Brunhilda, and they had two children, Princess Blossom and Prince Bruce. The king was not cruel and most of the time he was quite friendly. And as long as he got his way, he did not get angry.

Like other members of his family, King Boris did not do very much. They all ate and slept much of the time. Often the King and Queen would play cards with each other and gamble small amounts of money. But sometimes Queen Brunhilda would catch King Boris cheating. They loved playing cards and King Boris had a sense of fun. He hated all the ceremonies of state, but he had to attend them because they were part of his job. Every day Prince Bruce would play with his toys, and Princess Blossom would slowly comb her own long hair and play with dolls. Because of their inactive lives, they all got rather fat, especially the two children.

Princess Blossom owned a horse and once wanted to go horse-riding. But she found it easier to feed it with treats, and the horse became too lazy. Prince Bruce wanted to be a soldier one day. He found an old uniform in a dusty palace wardrobe. But when he tried to put it on it was too small for him, and three of the buttons popped off near his waist. He tried marching but gave up after one minute: he felt too puffed and tired and did not want to carry on. So he went back into the palace and played with his toy soldiers instead.

King Boris had a Prime Minister and other assistants. There were few problems in the kingdom, and nothing much ever changed. The Prime Minister was meant to meet the king twice a week and make a report on what was happening in the kingdom. But because not very much extraordinary happened, they often forgot about these meetings. Because there was not much work to do, the Prime Minister, the scribe and the other assistants often took days off work. They took picnics by the lake or went to the pub for a drink of bubbly bitter beer, which made them burp all day long. Otherwise they stayed at home and ate big tasty meals such as roast chicken or macaroni cheese, cooked by their servants.

There were few noble families who had inherited wealth from their ancestors. These lords and ladies owned big mansions and did not do much work. Then there were the landowners, who lived off the rent they took from the peasant farmers. They too did not do much work, but they had plenty of money to spend. Then there was a blacksmith who put shoes on the horses. There was a miller, who made flour from the grain that was grown by the farmers, and made a nice profit from the service. There was a baker who made bread from the flour. He charged a bit too much for his bread, but nobody protested and nobody was without food.

There were many servants, who looked after the rich people and their homes. They cleaned and cooked, and brought the rich people what they wanted. Then there were the peasant farmers. They worked harder than everyone else. They grew crops and looked after animals. The land was mostly fertile and they always had enough to eat, but they were still poor and could not afford to take much time off work. There was always something that needed doing.

After taking what they needed to feed themselves, they sold most of the rest of their produce in the local market, and they made just enough money to pay the rent to the landowners. In years when the harvest was good they would store grain in the great village storehouse, which all the farmers had built together, many years before. This ensured that they would have enough to eat in a following year if the weather was poor and the harvest was bad. After the harvest, the wives would bottle fruit and vegetables in storage jars to get their families through the winter.

That is the way the kingdom worked, year after year. Everyone knew their rank and place in society, and what (if anything) they had to do. Everyone had enough for their basic needs. Although some people had more than others, nobody grumbled or made a fuss. There were no newspapers, because there was never any news. Radio and television had not yet been invented.

There was no need for a democracy or a parliament because no-one wanted to change anything or make any new laws. From the king down to the peasant farmers, everyone was more-or-less happy as things were.

Long ago, the royal ancestors of King Boris had ordered that all the laws be written down in one book. Things were going so well in the kingdom and everyone was mostly happy, so they wanted all the rules and laws recorded, so that they could last forever.

So the scribe who worked for the ancestor of King Boris wrote down a *Book of Laws*. The book had many pages, and every law and custom was written down very neatly and carefully using a quill pen and a pot of ink. After doing his work for many long days, and getting very tired because he did not get enough sleep, the scribe had an accident when he finished the book. He fell asleep at his desk and spilt some ink on the title page of *The Book of Laws*. But this was not its full title.

The book had a longer title: *The Book of Laws of the Land of* ▬. But the scribe had spilt ink on the name of the country, and so it was forgotten. People reading the book did not want to say '*The Book of Laws of the Land of Ink-blob*' or '*The Book of Laws of the Land of Messy-bit-on-the-page*' or '*The Book of Laws of the Land of Oh Dear I Can't Read What Comes Next*', so they just referred to the long document as *The Book of Laws*.

This very heavy and important *Book of Laws* – which had taken the scribe so long to write out – was locked away in a safe place in a chest in the king's palace. But because very little in the kingdom ever changed, and extraordinary things rarely happened, they did not refer to the book very often. The Prime Minister and his assistants remembered many of the laws and rules, or at least enough of them to make the people think that they were doing very important work as officials, and for the king to keep them in their jobs. And when the Prime Minister and his assistants did not know some of the laws, they just pretended that they did. No-one ever challenged them and tried to find the actual *Book of Laws,* to check if they knew what they were talking about.

So eventually the king and the other people in the palace even forgot the place where *The Book of Laws* was kept. The palace cleaners were a bit lazy because the king and queen rarely bothered about the dust and dirt in the many rooms in the palace that they never visited. So the cleaners never found the book either. It never seemed to matter that everyone had forgotten where it was.

Also it did not matter much that people forgot the name of their own country. It had few visitors and it never went to war. Its small population lived in the middle of an island, far away from other countries. This island had fields, lakes, hills, mountains and lots of uninhabited moorland.

Some people argue that things without names cannot exist, so this country did not ever exist. But that's a bit silly, because things existed before humans evolved and developed a language and gave things names. If things did not exist when they did not have names, then humans could not have evolved.

But many more people argue that there is no evidence for this country without a name other than in stories. So it did not really exist. But it *does*. Not only did it exist *then*, but it exists *now*.

Just close your eyes firmly and then imagine King Boris and Queen Brunhilda playing cards and Princess Blossom and Prince Bruce all in their palace … and *The Book of Laws* (with the ink blob on the title page) hidden inside a chest … and the Prime Minister and his assistants … and the landowners in the pub … and the miller, the blacksmith, and the baker … and the farmers working in the fields with the hills just visible far away in the distance. Can you see them all? If not, then you must try harder, because unless you can see them you will not really understand what happened next. Can you see them now? You can? Then they *must* really exist.

So what do you think happened next?

2. Odd-Numbered April Fools' Days

There were some laws that *everyone* remembered. Every year there were some special days, like holidays, days of celebration, days of commemoration, harvest festivals and the like. The scribe who had written out *The Book of Laws* had listed long ago all these special days, and had written down what was meant to happen on each of them. He had done a very thorough job in recording all the customs and turning them into laws. (Because he worked so hard he got tired and spilled ink on the title page.)

The laws concerning 'Special Days' were written down in Chapter 43 of *The Book of Laws*. Section 15 of this chapter was titled 'Laws Concerning the First Day of April, Otherwise Known as "April Fools' Day"'. And in this section there were listed a number of Articles with rules to be followed on that day.

These rules were a bit complicated, because there were different sets of rules for odd-numbered and even-numbered years. Repeating here all the actual rules would be a bit boring, because they were written in the kind of formal and tedious language often used by scribes and lawyers and university professors, and other people who want to seem very important, and want other people to think that they know much more than they really do. They use difficult language to make them seem cleverer than they really are. In any case, everyone remembered these particular rules and there was no need to find *The Book of Laws* on each first day of April. They remembered these rules because on the first day of April every year they had so much fun.

Every year, when the first day of April arrived, everyone would get up early at six-o'clock. They would all wash and have a quick breakfast to gather on the lawn in front of the king's palace at eight-o'clock. The king would then appear. After a short fanfare by two trumpeters he would give a short speech. 'Welcome, my subjects,' he would say. 'According to the ancient customs and laws of our great and glorious nation we together shall celebrate April Fool's Day!' Everyone would cheer and the men would throw their hats into the air.

Then the king would briefly explain what was to happen that year. For example, he would say: 'Today we are in the seventh year of my glorious reign, so it is an odd-numbered year!' The people would cheer again. (Some mothers or fathers would explain to very young children – sometimes using an odd number of coins, toy bricks or short sticks to show this – that if you divide an odd number by two, then it always leaves a remainder of one. But I am sure that *you* know that already.)

The king would then continue: 'According to *The Book of Laws,* on odd-numbered years in the reign of a king, men and women, girls and boys, shall each *swap places.* Husbands will dress up in their wives' clothes and do the jobs normally done by the wives. Wives shall dress up in their husband's clothes and do the jobs normally done by the husbands. Brothers shall dress up in their sisters' clothes and play with their sisters' toys. Sisters shall dress up in their brothers' clothes and play with their brothers'

toys.' Everyone would then laugh. The king would say: 'Go back to your homes and jobs, my kind subjects, and enjoy this special day!' The people would cheer again and then go back to their homes and swap roles.

The king did not say what would happen if a man or woman were living together but unmarried, or if a man or a woman were living alone, or two men or two women were living together, or if there were families with more brothers than sisters or more sisters than brothers. He said nothing about these cases. In fact, these cases were not considered in *The Book of Laws*. But no-one bothered to object. The single men and women, and the same-sex couples, and the brothers without sisters, and the sisters without brothers all had so much fun that day watching everyone else that they did not bother to make a fuss. And they did not have to swap their clothes. No-one asked whether these special cases were actually covered by *The Book of Laws*. Everyone enjoyed themselves so much.

So men and women, and boys and girls, swapped clothes according to the king's instructions and they followed the rules in *The Book of Laws*. This led to much fun. Often the clothes would not fit. One fat wife's dress would be far too big for her skinny husband. One tall husband's trousers would be far too long and big for his short and slim wife. The men and the women would go

12

onto the street in their ill-fitting clothes. The neighbours would burst out laughing and make jokes about how they looked.

Young children would sometimes get upset swapping their clothes. Many of them did not like to look silly. But their parents would then say: 'Come on children, don't be upset. Don't be embarrassed. Look, all the adults have swapped clothes and are having great fun. It is a very special day today when we follow the customs of our great kingdom. Why don't you join in?' Many of the children would then swap their clothes like the rest. Older children would learn to take pride in following this ancient April Fools' Day custom. The older boys would strut about in dresses and even put on lipstick and other make-up. The older girls would have fun acting like boys and mocking their pomposity or bossiness.

If the very young children really insisted that they did not want to swap clothes because they felt too embarrassed, then their parents would say: 'Never mind, when you are much bigger in two years' time then I am sure you want to join in the fun, like all the others.' And if brothers and sisters did swap clothes, and then argue because each was playing with toys normally belonging to the other, then their parents would say: 'Don't argue children, this is just a bit of fun. You will have your normal toys back tomorrow.'

And by mid-morning, if the adults had not split their sides laughing at each other too much, they would all try and go out and do some work. But then there would be more fun. Some could not even walk properly because the clothes were too tight. Some short men would trip up with the long dresses they were wearing, and fall into the mud.

Some women had no idea how to do the jobs normally done by their husbands. The miller's wife tried to grind the corn but had no idea how to operate the machinery. Many husbands tried to do the cooking and cleaning, but the meals often tasted awful and the houses got even messier and dirtier. They all laughed at each other.

In the king's palace, there was just as much fun. The king and queen would swap clothes, and laugh at each other. Queen Brunhilda would put on the king's crown and sit on the throne for a while, but then get bored and come down again. The queen would try and cheat at cards, but King Boris would then say: 'you are a little cheaty-weety' and they would both laugh again and play cards and gamble a bit more. King Boris would also suggest that they acted out their parts in short plays that he would write specially for the occasion. He found the idea of a man playing a woman and a woman playing a man very funny.

Dressed up in his sister's clothes, Prince Bruce went to the stable to get onto Princess Blossom's horse, but the stable boy had gone to watch the fun in the town, and he had no sister to replace him, so there was no-one else to lift the heavy saddle onto the large horse. So Prince Bruce went back into the palace and got very bored combing his own hair. Meanwhile Princess Blossom got bored playing with soldiers and went to sleep.

A few people did not gain much enjoyment from the day. The Prime Minister swapped clothes with wife, but he then refused to go out in public. His wife tried doing his job but discovered that there was not very much to do.

By the evening, everyone in the town was in a good mood. Many of them went down to the pub. They sang songs and drank lots of beer. But all the children and many of their parents were so tired after the fun that they were already in bed. They knew that next day everything would go back to normal. They all slept very soundly.

That is how everyone in the kingdom celebrated April Fools' days on *odd*-numbered years. What do you think they did on *even*-numbered years? It was very different, and it shall be explained in the next chapter.

3. An Even-Numbered April Fools' Day

What happened on the first day of April on even-numbered years? As before, when the first day of April arrived, everyone would get up early at six-o'clock. They would all wash and have a quick breakfast to gather on the lawn in front of the king's palace at eight-o'clock. The king would then appear. After a short fanfare by two trumpeters he would give a short speech. 'Welcome, my subjects,' he would say. 'According to the ancient customs and laws of our great and glorious nation we together shall celebrate April Fool's Day!' Everyone would cheer and the men would throw their hats into the air.

Then the king explained what was to happen that year. For example, he would say: 'Today we are in the eighth year of my glorious reign, so it is an even-numbered year!' The people would cheer again. (Some mothers or fathers would explain to very young children: if you divide an even number by two, then it always divides exactly, leaving no remainder. But I am sure that *you* know that already.)

From then on the rules were very different from odd-numbered years. For example, in the eighth year of the reign of King Boris he continued: 'According to *The Book of Laws,* on even-numbered years in the reign of a king, we all swap places according to rank. Please, kind people, line up in families according to your rank.'

The families would then all sort themselves out, according to rank. The first family was of course King Boris, Queen Brunhilda, Prince Bruce and Princess Blossom. Next were the other noble families, all lined up according to status. Next were the Prime minister and his wife, followed by the families of his assistants. Then came the landowners with their families. Group number twenty-nine was the miller and his wife, the blacksmith and his family were group thirty, the baker and his wife were group thirty-one and the rest were the families of the servants and the peasant farmers. This year there were sixty families in all.

The Prime Minister made an attempt to rank every family according to its status. Among the servants and the peasant farmers he put the families with most money first. But most of them had very little money so it was difficult to rank the very poor according to wealth. As the Prime Minister wasn't especially nice or fair, he often put the families that he decided looked most ugly or stupid in this final group.

The Prime Minister noted down the status or job of each family in order. Then he declared: 'Family number one will take over the role of family number sixty.' This meant that the royal family would take over the job of the lowest peasant family for a day. The Prime minister continued: 'And family number sixty will take the place of family number one.' This of course meant that the lowest peasant family would go to the palace and pretend to be the royal family for the day.

'Family number two will take over the role of family number fifty-nine.' This meant that the next-highest lord and lady in the land would become peasant farmers for the day. 'And family number fifty-nine will take the place of family number two.' All the highly-ranked people, down to the landlords and the miller's family, became servants in the rich houses or peasant farmers. The families of the blacksmith and the baker simply swapped places. Everyone below them – all the families or servants of peasant farmers – moved higher up the social ladder.

The couple that the Prime Minister thought to be most ugly and stupid became king and queen for the day. They were waited upon by servants who were really landowners or from noble families. A number of other poor peasants moved into the large and plush houses of the nobility, and were also waited upon by nobles or landowners. Some peasants and servants moved into the houses of the landowners, just for that day.

It was amazing to watch lords and ladies, who had not done much work in their lives, trying to farm and work in the fields. Their fine clothes got messy in the mud, and they had trouble lifting and using farm tools. But generally they regarded it as 'jolly good fun', and took it all in good humour. But soon they were heard to say: 'Thank goodness we have to do this for one day only.'

King Boris and Queen Brunhilda quickly decided that farm work was not for them. So they sat in the farmhouse and played cards and gambled for small amounts of money. Princess Blossom tried to get on a large farm horse, but it was very big and, after one try, she decided she could not mount it. So she sat in the porch and combed her hair. Prince Bruce had already got tired walking down to the farm, so he found a barn and fell asleep in the hay.

The blacksmith had taken over the job of the baker. He tried to bake some bread. He made the ovens far too hot and the bread was burned. Meanwhile the miller was trying to do the job of the blacksmith. After lifting hot and heavy metal and beating it with a large hammer for ten minutes, he felt exhausted. He went inside, and his wife made him some tea.

The peasants who occupied the houses owned by the landlords did not have much fun. They had been told that *The Book of Laws* decreed that rent shall always be collected on the last day of the month, without exception. That is when it was paid. But this day was the first day of the month, so they had nothing to do. Many of them said: 'It isn't much fun being a landlord.' Some even felt sorry for the landlords and their families, for having nothing interesting, useful or creative to do. There was also not much excitement for the peasant who took over the job of the Prime Minister for the day. There wasn't much to do, so he took his wife out for a picnic by the lake. They relaxed and enjoyed the day, and forgot about prime ministerial duties.

It was a bit more fun for the lower-ranked peasants, now sitting in the large houses of the noble families. The first thing that they would do would be to order the servants (who of course were really lords and ladies) to bring them things and do jobs for them. One peasant shouted at a servant: 'You! Bring me a cup of tea!' The servant-for-that-day brought up the teapot, cups and saucers and a few cakes. The peasant picked up a cake and rudely threw it at the servant: 'I didn't ask for this! Eat it yourself!' and then laughed out loud in a rough and coarse voice. The servant was not amused and glared at the peasant, as if to remind him of his true status and what might happen to him tomorrow if he misbehaved too much today.

The Prime Minister ordered the family that he thought was the ugliest and most stupid to be installed in the royal palace. The husband had a rough face and a protruding front tooth. The wife had untidy and straggly hair. They had rarely washed themselves. For a while they did not do much, except taking turns to sit on the king's throne. The wife thought hard and eventually remembered what she had been told of the food and drink of the rich. She plucked up courage and ordered a servant, in her best attempt at a posh voice: 'One would like some champagne and caviar. I mean, us *two* eere … my husband and I require caviar and champagne.' She made a gesture with her hand, causing her even-more-bashful husband to laugh and coarsely remark: 'Hi queeny – ha, ha, ha.'

The caviar and champagne arrived. They tried the tiny fish eggs and said: 'Ee-er what's this, then?' And then, after a few minutes of tasting: 'Can't see wot all the fuss is about.' 'It don't beat egg and chips.' So they drank the bubbly champagne, burped loudly a few times, and fell asleep on the sofa.

At the appointed hour of eight o'clock in the evening, everyone would go back to their real homes and assume their former positions in society. The noble families with their muddied clothes would walk up the lane together, and meet groups of peasants coming in the opposite direction. 'Jolly good fun, what!' the nobles would say. And the peasants would tip their hats and reply: 'Yes my lord … Yes my lady. … Glad you enjoyed your day, sir. … Pleased you enjoyed your day, madam.'

And in a couple of hours they all would be sound asleep in their real homes, and the next day everything would have returned to normal.

But many people really thought that April Fools' days in even-numbered years were not as much fun as those in odd-numbered years. Some even complained to the Prime Minister, who once went to the king to raise the topic.

But the king would have none of it. 'How dare you suggest that we should deviate from *The Book of Laws?*' he shouted angrily. 'Do you want to keep your job? If not I shall find some who really wants to uphold our ancient customs and laws.' So the Prime Minister never raised the topic with King Boris again.

But the king really cared more about himself. He enjoyed going down to a farmhouse for a few hours. For one day every two years he would get away from the large, boring and dusty palace with too many servants, if only to play cards and gamble a little money with the queen. Sometimes he found simple games like darts and draughts in the peasant's houses, and he would play these with her. But most of all it amused him to see the nobles getting all muddy and pretending to enjoy the experience. He did not like the other nobles very much, and it was great to see them briefly lowered in status and humiliated.

But no-one – including the people who found April Fools' days in even-numbered years boring – had any idea what was going to happen a few years later. It was going to be much more exciting. We shall see what happened in the next part of the story.

4. April Fools' Day in the Sixteenth Year of King Boris

Several years passed and things went on as before. On all days in the year except one, people would assume their position in society and do the job that corresponded with their sex and their rank. The disruption on each April Fools' Day was often fun, and it served to remind everyone that everything had its proper place. So by the second of April every year, everyone had gone back to their proper position in society, and they did the things that they were supposed to do.

King Boris remained on the throne and nothing much else happened. He had got slightly fatter and had acquired some grey hairs. Princess Blossom and Prince Bruce were then both in their early twenties, but neither had married. Sadly some old people in the kingdom had died. But several delightful little babies had been born. Some peasant families had become a little bit richer and some had got a bit poorer, depending on how hard they had worked and on the luck of the harvests. Apart from that, nothing much had changed.

Then it came round to the first day of April once again. Everyone got up early at six-o'clock. They all washed and have a quick breakfast to gather on the lawn in front of the king's palace at eight-o'clock. King Boris appeared. There was a short fanfare by two trumpeters. But King Boris had forgotten his spectacles, which he now needed for reading, so there was a short delay while a servant went into the palace to find them. The spectacles were quickly found, and King Boris put them on to read from his notes.

After a repeat fanfare by two trumpeters he gave his short speech. 'Welcome, my subjects,' he said. 'According to the ancient customs and laws of our great and glorious nation we together shall celebrate April Fool's Day!' Everyone cheered and the men threw their hats into the air.

Then the king explained: 'Today we are in the sixteenth year of my long and glorious reign, so it is an even-numbered year!' The people would cheer again. (Some mothers or fathers would explain to very young children: if you divide an even number by two, then it always divides exactly, leaving no remainder. But *you* know that already.)

King Boris continued: 'According to *The Book of Laws,* on even-numbered years in the reign of a king, we all swap places according to rank. Please, kind people, line up in families according to your rank.'

The families then all sorted themselves out according to rank. The first family consisted of course of King Boris, Queen Brunhilda, Prince Bruce and Princess Blossom. Next were the other noble families, all lined up according to status. Next were the Prime minister and his wife, followed by the families of his assistants. Then came the landowners and their families, then the miller and his wife, then the blacksmith and his family, then the baker and his wife, and then the families of the servants and the peasant farmers. There were sixty families in all. They were roughly, but not entirely, in the same order as before. Some people had died, and some families had got a little bit richer or a little bit poorer.

The Prime Minister made sure that every family was ranked according to its status. Among the servants and the peasant farmers he put the families with most money first. But most of them had very little money so it was difficult to rank the very poor according to wealth. So in this final group he often put the families that looked most ugly or stupid.

The Prime Minister noted down the status or job of each family in order. Then he declared: 'Family number one will take over the role of family number sixty.' This meant that the royal family would take over the job of the lowest peasant family for a day. The Prime minister continued:

'And family number sixty will take the place of family number one.' This of course meant that the lowest peasant family would go to the palace and pretend to be the royal family for the day.

'Family number two will take over the role of family number fifty-nine.' This meant that the next-highest lord and lady in the land would become peasant farmers for the day. 'And family number fifty-nine will take the place of family number two.' All the highly-ranked people, down to the landlords and the miller's family, would become servants in the rich houses or peasant farmers. The families of the blacksmith and the baker would simply swap places. Everyone below them would move higher up the social ladder.

But the order among the lowest families had changed a little. This year, the lowest ranked family was of ordinary peasant farmers called Albert and Agnes, with their little eight-year-old daughter Annie. Just after Annie was born, her mother Agnes had got sick. So Albert had to take time off work to look after her. He did not have time to tend properly to his crops and he found it difficult to pay the rent and make ends meet.

His landlord allowed him to delay paying the rent for a while, but charged him massive interest at ten per cent a month. The rent was ten silver crown coins every month. In just five months, with the interest added, Albert owed the landlord over sixty-one crowns.

Times were tough for Albert and Agnes, but they worked hard, sold off some of their furniture and eventually paid the landlord all that they owed. But because of the very high rates of interest they were much poorer than before.

While ranking the family of Albert and Agnes, the Prime Minister noticed that they were both very short in height, and neither was very handsome. The Prime Minister concluded that they must be stupid as well as short, and placed them in the lowest rank of all.

So Albert and Agnes and their daughter Annie moved into the royal palace for the day. Everyone else in the kingdom changed places too. Soon the king and queen would be playing cards in Albert's and Agnes's farmhouse. Eventually the nobles would get dirty in the fields, the peasants would get bored in the houses of the landlords, and the blacksmith would burn the bread in the baker's oven.

When Albert arrived in the palace he immediately climbed up to sit upon the king's throne. He had very short legs and they dangled without touching the floor. He looked very small on the large throne. He put the king's crown on his head. This made him look even smaller.

He did not order his servants to bring him champagne or caviar. He did not ask for egg and chips. He did not even order a cup of tea. Instead, he shouted, in a clear and determined tone, and in such a big and firm voice for a very little man:

'Bring me *The Book of Laws!*'

'Er … yes sire,' the servant (who was really a lord) answered, 'right away sire'. So he and a few other servants (who really were lords or landlords) went off to look for the book. They enquired where it was, but no-one was sure. So they looked around the palace, but it could not be found. They returned to the king and explained that the book was nowhere to be seen.

King Albert responded. 'So where are written down the laws that say that you are entitled to your lands, your privileges and your titles. By what law are you called "*lord* this" and "*lady* that"? Do you want to keep your titles and your privileges? And those of you who are landlords, by what law do you have the right to own the land and charge a rent? When we go back to our normal positions after today, do you want it known throughout the kingdom that the laws that keep you in power and keep you rich cannot be found, or that they do not really exist?

So bring me *The Book of Laws!*'

The lords and ladies then tried a lot harder to find the book. They were worried about their wealth and privileges. Eventually – but it took them a long time to think of this – one of them had the sense to go out of the palace and look some of the real servants who normally worked in the king's home. They found two of them in one of the landlord's houses, lounging on the sofa. The woman thought long and then answered that she had heard somewhere that *The Book of Laws* was locked up safely in a chest in the palace. But she did not know where that chest was, or where to find the key.

By this time it was past lunchtime. But King Albert was not bothered by food and he still sat firmly on the throne. Then the two servants (who really were lords) returned. They explained to Albert that that had tracked down some real servants who had said that the book did really exist, but it was locked up in a chest somewhere in the palace. So his highness need not worry. They had clear information that the laws really did exist and were written down somewhere. 'Everything is in order. Is there anything else you require, sire?'

'So *where* is this chest in which the book is locked?' Albert retorted.

'Alas we are unsure, sire. But rest assured, it is somewhere in the palace. It does really exist. Everything is in order.' Albert glared at them. 'Then go find it!' said Albert.

'Bring me *The Book of Laws!* '

The servants rushed off, and twenty minutes later several of them returned. 'We have found many chests, sire. We searched inside those that are open, without finding the book. But many other chests are locked and we cannot find the keys.'

'Then force them open!' said Albert. 'But there are so many, sire', was the reply. Albert said for the fourth and last time:

'Bring me *The Book of Laws!* '

The servants searched high and low, not daring to return to Albert before they had found it. They forced open many chests, but without any success. Several hours passed and it became late afternoon. Everyone was becoming worried that the book would not be found. Secretly, and to himself, Albert was the most worried of all.

What do you think happened? To find out, you must read the next chapter.

5. Where was *The Book of Laws?*

Albert was in a very difficult position. He had taken a big risk and assumed that the book would be found. He would be very embarrassed if it were not found that day. But hours had passed and no-one had found it. What would he do if they all failed?

Then one servant decided to look in the attic. It was full of junk, all covered in dust. But in one corner was an old chest. It was dirty and chipped. The servant forced it open with a crowbar. There inside she found the large and ancient *Book of Laws,* resting uncared for and covered in dirt and dust. Quickly the servant brushed off some of the dust and dirt and saw the words on the cover: *The Book of Laws.* Inside it said: *The Book of Laws of the Land of* ▬▬▬ .

She rushed as fast as she could down to the throne room, struggling with the large and heavy book, and declared to Albert: 'I've found it sire! Here it is!'

Albert got down from his throne and looked the servant in the eye: 'Thank you. You shall be a noble lady tomorrow.' But the servant (who was really a lady) was puzzled and thought to herself: 'What *does* he mean? Everyone knows that I shall be a noble lady again tomorrow, when we have changed back to our normal positions.'

But Albert had other ideas. He asked for the large and heavy book to be placed on a table in the next room. He opened the book and inspected its list of contents. He had learned to read when he was a boy, but he was not used to reading, and he read quite slowly. Sure enough, there were laws about everything. Among them was a list of noble titles and privileges. The rights of landlords to charge rents to the farmers and interest on loans were set out in detail. There was even a survey of the kingdom. It identified the families who owned each piece of land. The very first law in the book was Article 1. It read: 'No existing law in this book may ever be changed.' For an hour or more, Albert pored over the book. And everyone was mystified as to his purpose. No-one knew what he was up to.

Then Albert turned to the last page with writing in the book. Following this last written page there were several more blank pages. The last words of writing were: 'Chapter 139. Space here for new laws – but no new law may overturn any previous law.' So at the beginning and end of the book it made clear that nothing could be changed. New laws could be added, but they must not contradict any existing law.

Albert thought again and turned back to Section 15 of Chapter 43, titled 'Laws Concerning the First Day of April, Otherwise Known as "April Fools' Day"'. In this section there were listed a number of Articles with rules to be followed on that day. But by this time the sun was low in the sky, and the day was nearly at an end. Soon everyone would have to return to their proper places.

Albert read Section 15 of Chapter 43 slowly and very carefully. It explained what would happen on April Fools' Days on odd-numbered years, and what would happen on April Fools' Days on even-numbered years. Everything was set out in great detail. Nothing was out of order. He read out some of the articles to his daughter Annie, who had joined him at the table. Article 74 of Section 15 of Chapter 43 said: 'People shall change their social positions as detailed above. These changes made on April Fools' Day shall begin at eight o'clock in the morning and last unchanged until eight o'clock in the evening.' It was then six o'clock. Albert had only about two hours left.

Albert thought long and hard. He began to doubt his abilities and told himself that he wasn't clever enough to find a way to fix such a big mess. What could he do? No solution came to mind. Then Annie's face lit up: 'Daddy! It says "eight o'clock in the evening", but it does *not* say that everyone afterwards shall *return* to their places! Look daddy!'

'Bless me' said Albert 'you're right. Clever girl, Annie.' Just to make sure, he checked again. He tried to find all the places where April Fools' Day was mentioned. Nowhere did it say that people must return to the places or positions that they had occupied on the preceding day. Everyone had *assumed* that they should return to their places at eight o'clock in the evening, and they had all done so for many years, but nowhere was it actually written down in *The Book of Laws.* It did not actually say that everything or everyone had to return to normal.

Albert looked up at the servants in the room: 'Which of you can write, and who has the neatest handwriting?' One of them came forward. Albert then said to another servant: 'Go fetch a quill pen and ink.' Albert turned to the last page on which there was handwriting. 'Write this down here' he instructed. Albert dictated slowly:

'First Article made on first day of April, which began in the sixteenth year of the Reign of King Boris. By instruction of the former King Boris, I, Albert have assumed the title of king on this day until eight o'clock in the evening. Without contracting anything in *The Book of Laws,* I shall remain as king *after* eight o'clock this evening. With my rightful authority as king I hereby declare that King Boris shall *never* be king again. He shall retire and live on the farmhouse I used to occupy with my wife Agnes and daughter Annie just over the river and just beyond the town.' He then waited for a while so that the scribe could catch up, putting everything down in his nice neat handwriting.

Albert then continued: 'Second Article made on first day of April, which began in the sixteenth year of the Reign of King Boris. After eight o'clock in the evening on *future* April Fools' Days, everyone shall return to the place and rank that they occupied before eight o'clock in the morning on that same day. I am King Albert, my wife is Queen Agnes, and my daughter is Princess Annie.' He then waited a while for all this to be written down in *The Book of Laws.* All the servants looked very shocked.

Princess Annie whispered in his ear: 'Daddy, you've forgotten something.' Albert then said: 'Oh yes,' please continue with these words: 'The only exception to the above is the lady who has found *The Book of Laws* today. For her great service to the kingdom, she alone may return to the position, title and home that she occupied yesterday. There shall be no other exceptions to this rule.' The servant added those words as instructed, and King Albert signed the new law.

'Thank you, King Albert', said the servant (who *really* was a lady) who had found the book. She was much relieved that she alone, among all the lords and ladies, would return to her large and stately home.

Then King Albert instructed all the servants to travel to the town and to all the farms and explain that they should all remain where they were. Many people protested. But the servants explained about the new law. By this time it was dark and everyone was tired and wanted to go bed, even if it did not seem their own. So they all slept in unfamiliar bedrooms. Many of the beds in the houses of the peasants were hard, or uncomfortable, or even had bugs or fleas. The former royal family and the former nobles were not used to these rough conditions. They had an uncomfortable and itchy night. But the people who were previously peasants had larger, cleaner and more comfortable beds. And they slept soundly and deeply the whole night long.

But could Albert remain king? We shall see later if he did.

6. Second Day in the Reign of King Albert

It was now the second day of April. It was a lovely spring day and some of the blossom was already on the trees. King Albert and Queen Agnes and Princess Annie had slept very well in the comfortable beds in the palace that night. But once they woke up they realised that their little world had been turned upside-down. They wondered if they had done right thing. But they remembered that they had broken none of the rules in *The Book of Laws*.

King Albert and Queen Agnes and Princess Annie went to one of the fine dining rooms in the large palace and rank the little brass bell that had been left on the table to call one of the servants. Eventually, after ringing the bell several times, a servant appeared, looking a bit dazed and confused. Eventually he got his wits together and said: 'Good morning your highnesses. May I be of service?'

King Albert, Queen Agnes and Princess Annie ordered poached eggs on buttered toast, and a pot of tea. It was as tasty a breakfast that they were used to in the farmhouse, and it was so much nicer to have it served to them and not have to do the washing-up afterwards. Then Albert said to Queen Agnes and Princess Annie: 'What shall we do today?' They no longer had jobs to do on the farm, so they weren't really sure.

Back on the farm, Boris (who used to be King Boris) had woken up in the farmhouse in a bad mood. The farmhouse bed was uncomfortable, Brunhilda had kept him awake with her snoring, and there was no other room with a bed that he could use instead. So he had moved out to the barn and had slept in the hay. When he awoke he felt very itchy. Blossom had slept badly in Annie's little bed. Bruce was the only one to have slept well.

Boris was hungry, so he went into the farmhouse kitchen. All he could find to eat was a half-eaten loaf of bread. He did not know how to boil an egg or make a cup of tea. Neither did Brunhilda, Blossom nor Bruce. So they cut the bread into four and chewed it slowly, each in an irritable mood and with a glum face.

When he had eaten, Boris declared to his wife: 'What happened yesterday is *outrageous*. I'm going to find the Prime Minister and sort all this out.' So off he went up the road. Eventually he found the former Prime Minister in another peasant farmhouse.

The former Prime Minister was also in a bad mood. They discussed frantically how to get things back to normal. Eventually they decided to gather together with a few of the former Prime Minister's former assistants and go up to the royal palace.

An hour or so later, Boris, the former Prime Minister, and three former assistants strode up towards the royal palace. But they got a bit puffed on the way, so that had to take a ten-minute break to regain their breath. Then they strode up towards the palace again.

Boris marched into the palace and said loudly to a servant: 'Let me in! I am your king. I demand to see that impudent peasant Albert!' The servant (who had been a lord just two days before) wasn't quite sure how to react. Should he acknowledge Boris as his true sovereign, or insist that Albert was now king? Eventually he played safe and did neither, saying: 'Oh I am so glad to see you, do come in.'

Boris and the others tramped into a large palace room and found King Albert, who was seated at a table with Annie, reading state papers. Boris thundered: 'What is the meaning of all this? It is outrageous! You have disobeyed our ancient laws. Go back instantly to your farm! If you and your family go back right now, we shall forget about this little episode and there shall be not punishment. But *if you refuse,* then your punishment shall be most severe. It will be so severe that I shall have to spend the whole day thinking of all the many horrible things that will be done to you *before* you are hanged for treason. So go back to your farm immediately!'

The former Prime Minister and his former assistants nodded in endorsement, all thinking that this was a just the right kind of thing to say in the circumstances.

Then Albert replied: 'I do *not* refuse; I obey ...'

'So let *that* be the end of it,' interrupted Boris. 'It was all jolly good fun, but go back to your little peasant farm, right now!'

'Kindly allow me to continue,' Albert said. 'I do *not* refuse; I obey *The Book of Laws.*' He then pointed at the book, which was still on the table: 'If you can find a law

44

in that book that instructs me, or anyone else in my position, to go back to the place that I occupied before eight o'clock in the morning on the first day of April, then I shall go right away. I shall not refuse. And my family shall come with me.'

So Boris and the former Prime Minister and his former advisors gathered around the table and started reading *The Book of Laws*. At first they were sure that they would find such a law requiring Albert and his family to return to their farm, and everything would soon return to normal. It had happened that way at eight o'clock in the evening on the first day of April on every year in the past. So there must be a law to oblige everyone to return to their former positions.

But they looked long and hard, and they could not find such a law. After an hour of searching, Queen Agnes said: 'Would you all like to take a break and have a cup of tea?' But Boris and the others had forgotten their manners. None of them said: 'Yes please.' One of them just said 'OK.' So a servant was instructed, and after a few minutes a pot of tea and some cakes arrived.

When the tea and cakes arrived, Boris, the former Prime Minister and his former advisors all turned round and helped themselves. They all were hungry and had missed their cup of tea that morning. So they rudely crammed the cakes in their mouths and gulped down the tea.

Briefly satisfied, they then returned to *The Book of Laws*. They searched and searched, for another two hours. King Albert then declared: 'Well, have you found anything?' They shook their heads. 'Then return to your homes!'

Boris took the former Prime Minister to one side and said in a low voice that no-one else could hear: 'Prime Minister, we must think about this carefully. We need a plan to get rid of this traitor. Let us go back for now and devise a plan to sort out this mess. For now, I'll pretend to accept things as they are. Later we'll get hold of this dwarf – this vertically challenged upstart – and then clap him in irons.' The former Prime Minister agreed.

Boris then turned to King Albert, and said in a much louder voice: 'We have found no law that says I should return to the throne.' He then muttered to himself: 'But we might yet.' And then louder: 'We shall now leave the palace.'

Boris and the others left and returned to their homes. That evening, Boris and the former Prime Minister sat down together in front of a farmhouse fire, each drinking a cup of cold spring water from an old chipped cup. They talked for several hours about what could be done to put Boris back onto the throne and turn the world the right way up again. They talked for long, but they could not think of a good plan.

Eventually they got tired and returned to their beds. That night Brunhilda did not snore, so Boris slept a little bit better. Bruce had made a more comfortable bed for himself in the barn and Blossom was already fast asleep. Boris got a bit more used to the farmhouse bed, and he was exhausted by his walk to and from the palace, so he slept more soundly than on the preceding night. Meanwhile, King Albert, Queen Agnes and Princess Annie all slept very well indeed.

But not everything went well, as we shall see in the next chapter.

7. Crisis in the Reign of King Albert

Many of the former nobles and landlords all got a bit more used to sleeping in farmhouse beds. But otherwise things were not going well. They did not know how to plough the fields or plant crops. After they had eaten all the bread, meat and vegetables that had been left by the former tenants, they had nothing left in their houses except the bottled fruit and vegetables in storage jars. Eating these every day was tedious. But they had no alternative. Otherwise they would go hungry.

Some of them remembered how to hunt, so they found some of the farmer's guns and went into the woods and shot at a few birds. But they often missed their target.

Few of them knew how cook the birds. Some tried boiling them whole with their feathers still on. Cooked this way, these birds tasted awful and they made the peasants sick. They realised that their food was beginning to run out, so each family began to ration it very carefully.

After a couple of weeks they had run out of ammunition, and they did not have any money to buy any more. So they couldn't even eat birds.

At first, the former peasants in the fine houses had a great time. Their servants (who previously had been lords, ladies or landlords) eventually learned to cook a few basic dishes of food. So the former peasants in the fine houses had a comfortable life and ate quite well.

But after a week or so, some of the servants would come back from the market to their masters or mistresses and report that prices had being going up and up, and had reached very high levels. The peasants were bringing less and less produce to market. The servants complained to their masters and mistresses that they needed more money to pay for everything. This worried the new lords and ladies and landowners, but there was still quite a lot of money in their houses, so for a while they could pay. But market prices continued to rise rapidly. They reached levels one-hundred times above what they had been a few weeks before. Potatoes that were formerly sold at one silver crown coin for a large basket now cost one-hundred crowns. Few could afford to pay at these prices.

A few days later the markets closed, because no-one was bringing anything to sell and less and less people could afford to buy. The little fresh food that was being produced was consumed by the families who produced it. There was nothing spare to sell on the market.

By the end of the third week of April, things were bad for everyone. Food was scarce, and what could be found was expensive. These problems were reported to the king. On hearing this, King Albert was unsure what to do. He had thought that the former nobles and landlords would eventually learn to be peasant farmers and grow crops. But most of them had no idea. They were useless. They hadn't done a day's work in their lives.

King Albert decided to tour his kingdom and find out what was happening. He mounted his horse in new fine clothes that had been made for him in the palace, and he took with him a few of his servants and officials. Some of the people lined up by the side of the road and said: 'Long live King Albert!' In truth they were not very happy, and they did not greet King Albert with great enthusiasm, but they respected the laws of their country, even in times of exceptional difficulty. They said to one another that it was not King Albert's fault that the peasant farmers were useless at their jobs and had no idea how to farm.

King Albert discovered that on the farms very little spare food was being produced. Some of the new peasant farmers had learned how to grow a few things, but most of the others were stubborn or stupid, or both. He really had expected more of them. When he had been a peasant farmer, he and the others had managed to grow enough food for most of the time, and they hadn't had the luxury of a fine education. In contrast, the landowners and nobles had been to fee-paying schools for the rich, or had had their own personal tutors. Surely they should be able to manage shouldn't they, with all their knowledge and learning? But it was clear on this day that they could not manage. It would take them a long time to learn, if they ever did.

Finally, King Albert visited the blacksmith, the miller and the baker, and found out what was happening there. He completed his tour.

Late in the day, when the sun was setting on the horizon, King Albert and his retinue arrived back at the palace. He was very worried: he would spend the next day working out what could be done.

The following day, King Albert got up and started to work on the problems in his kingdom right away.

But meanwhile, down on the farms, the king's visit on the preceding day had stirred the peasants (who previously were lords or landlords) into action. Most importantly, in a few days' time it would be the end of the month. Rent would be due to the new landlords. They had no money to pay the rent. They got so upset that they rushed down to Boris's house and demanded a meeting.

One of the peasants said to Boris: 'Did you know that in a few days' time we all have to pay rent to those fake upstart landlords?' Boris did not realise that he had to pay rent, so he got agitated too. Another peasant shouted: 'And if we can't pay then they will charge us interest at ten per cent a month!'

'Ten per cent a month!' said Boris, 'That's outrageous! It must be against the law! It's far too high!'

'It is not, sire,' whispered another peasant in his ear, 'it's allowed in *The Book of Laws.*'

'But what can be done?' said Boris. 'Come inside, and we'll sort out all of this, once and for all.'

They argued for hours. No-one came up with a good idea. Then one of them said: 'Things are desperate. We are all starving. If nothing is done then things will only get worse. We must overthrow Albert by force of arms.'

One of them objected: 'But that's against the rules in *The Book of Laws!* My grandfather told me that it does not allow for revolution, and it says that traitors will be punished by death. My grandfather told me that, many centuries ago, a lord had tried to revolt against the king, and this lord had been convicted of treason and hanged.' Others nodded their heads in agreement.'

'So do you want to starve to death instead?' said the peasant who had suggested using force. 'Surely a quick death on the gallows is better than a long slow death by starvation, watching your wives and children dying slowly around you. You men are lords of our great nation, with its great history. Your ancestors were fighters and heroes. Let us march together on the palace tomorrow, for freedom, justice, nice food, and putting everything back into its proper place!'

Eventually they were all persuaded to rise up against King Albert. They spent the rest of the evening in preparation for their revolt. But they had no uniforms, and the guns they had were without bullets.

'Never fear,' said the instigator, 'we shall gather pitchforks from our farms and first march through the town, where the rest of the people will join us. After that there will be little resistance. We shall be victorious tomorrow!'

So they found their pitchforks and resolved to get up extremely early, at five o'clock, to march on the town at six. They wanted to act before King Albert learned of their plot and had time to devise as counter-strategy. But King Albert was cleverer than he seemed, and he slept very soundly in his palace bed that night.

But soon, as we shall see, King Albert would have a big problem to deal with.

8. The Peasants' Revolt

The peasants on the morning of the twenty-eight of April woke up at five o'clock and washed their faces in spring water. There was no food, so they skipped breakfast. Husbands and wives joined in the revolt. They gathered their pitchforks and met together. But Brunhilda, Blossom and Bruce all thought it was too much effort. So Boris alone headed the column as he marched with the other peasants towards the town, as the sun slowly appeared above the horizon.

When they reached the town, most people were still in bed. 'Down with Albert!' the peasants chanted. 'Down with who?' was the response from a window. 'Do you mean King Albert?' asked another. After twenty minutes of chanting and making a noise in the town only a few of the townspeople had joined them. But they had 'crossed the Rubicon' as some scholars say, and they had to go on. So they marched on towards the palace, chanting as they went.

They were twenty-two in number. Even if they were fewer than expected, they would be much bigger than any force that Albert could muster. They would take the royal palace by surprise. So that day victory would surely be theirs. It would go down forever in history as a victory for justice, freedom, social order, common sense, and yummy food.

They reached the palace grounds and lined up in straight ranks facing the palace itself. 'Come out Albert!' they shouted, and waved their pitchforks in the air. Boris and the former Prime Minister stood together bravely in front.

Albert came out wearing his fine clothes and crown. He was accompanied by Queen Agnes and Princess Annie, all in their fine royal clothes. The Queen and the Princess stood to the right of the king, looking bravely back at the mob. On the king's left were the lady who had found *The Book of Laws* in the attic and two servants holding the book itself.

Observing the situation, Boris cried to King Albert: 'You have no army, so you must surrender. I am the true king.'

Albert replied to them all in a loud voice: 'Yes, I have no army. That is obvious. You may choose to march forward, take over the palace and install another king. But what then would happen to *The Book of Laws* that you see in front of you? You will have taken power by force, and not by right. You might depose me, yet I am a king according to the laws in this book. If you take power, then the laws here against treason and insurrection would have been broken. The book would have to be destroyed, because its laws were no longer being followed. Boris would then become an absolute ruler, bound by no law. He could do what he wanted, and dispossess whom he wanted. There would be no law to stop him. You would have to be constantly on your guard against that tyrant, to protect your wealth and your rights. He could imprison those of you whom he disliked, and without trial. Surely the open fields you occupy now are much better than starvation in gaol?'

Most of the nobles knew that Boris did not like them very much, so these words worried them a lot. Then Albert declared:

'*The Book of Laws* decrees that acts of treason or insurrection are punishable by death. I call upon you all to lay down you pitchforks. You who choose now to abandon this illegal and reckless revolt will immediately be pardoned by me of treason, and you may return safely to your homes. I ask those of you who choose now to abandon this unlawful revolt to move now over to that far corner of the lawn.'

He pointed to a far corner of the lawn, where nearby was a large cart covered by a sheet of canvas. Beside it were two servants. Eleven of the insurgents moved over to that corner. The numbers in revolt had been halved, but Boris and ten others still stood their ground on the lawn, looking determined and holding their pitchforks.

Boris looked around him and counted their number. 'There are still enough of us to take the royal palace.' He turned to Albert. 'I call upon you to surrender!'

Albert took little notice, and shouted: 'Take the covers off the cart!'

This was done, to reveal a huge pile of loaves, buns and cakes of many kinds. When King Albert had visited the miller and the baker the preceding day, he noticed that they had become quite good at their new jobs. The miller had learned how to mill the grain, and the baker no longer burned the bread. King Albert had told them of the great store of grain in the village, and had secretly arranged for some to be delivered to the miller. He milled the grain during the night and delivered the flour to the baker, who had baked loaves, buns and cakes and delivered them on a cart to the palace, even before the peasants had got up.

The smell from the cart was irresistible, and Boris and his little army were starving. The eleven defectors from the band of rebels were already tucking in to the deliciously fresh buns and cakes. The other eleven, who had stood their ground, smelled the fresh bread and turned around. They saw the others tucking in, and quickly became worried that all the food would be soon eaten. So two more of them defected, and ran towards the cart. Then they all went over except one, leaving Boris alone on the lawn.

Albert cried to Boris: 'You know what happens, according to *The Book of Laws,* to those convicted of treason. Boris thought about his position for two seconds. 'I surrender too!' he cried. And then he too rushed over to get something to eat.

'Phew!' said King Albert quietly to Queen Agnes, 'this might not have worked.' Later that evening, after the peasants had gone back home, King Albert, Queen Agnes and Princes Annie sat round and discussed the events of the day. Annie asked: 'What would have happened if Boris had won?'

Queen Agnes responded: 'I'm not sure what would have happened to us. But one thing is sure, he would have had to hide or destroy *The Book of Laws*. He had broken the law and committed treason, so he would have had to hide from everyone that law and its decreed punishment.'

'But would Boris have really locked up all the nobles in the dungeon, as daddy said he would?' Annie asked.

'No of course not,' the queen replied. 'Boris is sometimes silly but not that stupid. He would have only locked up a few, from time to time, to keep all the others scared and in their place.'

Albert then thought hard, and said: 'If the peasants today had realised that if they had won, then *The Book of Laws* would have to be destroyed or hidden away somewhere, then they might not have been threatened by my words. After they had won they would be able make new laws as they wished. They would declare that, for some made-up reason, their revolt was legal and not treason. None of them would be tried for treason because they would have won. It's as simple as that. But none of them had the sense to see.'

Albert thought a bit longer: 'Without our *Book of Laws,* treason can never win. Because if treason wins, then those who plotted it will no longer call it treason. They will find some reason to justify revolt and call it righteous and legal, and severely punish for treason anyone who says otherwise.'

But Albert knew that something had to be done. They had won today but the same trick would not work again. Something had to be done to restore the supply of food and make the people happy.

That would have to wait until tomorrow. They all had had a very eventful and stressful day and they needed a good night's rest. So they all went to bed and fell fast asleep.

Would Albert and Boris sort things out? We shall see in the next chapter.

9. King Albert and Boris Meet at the Palace

It was the twenty-ninth of April. First thing that morning, King Albert instructed a servant to go to Boris in the farm and invite him to the royal palace for lunch. On receiving this invitation, Boris was at first a bit worried that Albert would punish him. But then he remembered that he had been pardoned by Albert the day before. The thought of a fine lunch was irresistible. He hadn't eaten a good meal for four weeks.

On his walk towards the royal palace, Boris thought hard about what he should do. Revolution hadn't worked, so perhaps he should try using the law against Albert instead. What he needed was one of those clever lawyers. But because disputes had in the past been so rare, and everyone knew and accepted their place in society, no-one used lawyers, and they had all emigrated to other countries for work. Because of *The Book of Laws,* they did not need lawyers. But then Boris thought of an idea. Perhaps he could turn the tables on Albert after all.

Boris arrived alone at the palace at noon. He was welcomed in by a servant, who showed him to a waiting room. Boris paced up and down the room, thinking of his clever plan, or rather, thinking how clever he was to have such a plan. Thirty minutes passed. Then a servant entered the room and announced: 'luncheon is served.' Boris was escorted to the dining room, where King Albert, Queen Agnes and Princess Annie were already seated.

King Albert declared: 'Welcome Boris. Come sit down here beside me.' Boris did as he was asked. 'I hope we can both forget about our little dispute yesterday,' Albert remarked. Boris nodded, just as some servants entered the room and began serving the soup.

It was a humble leek and potato soup, but Boris thought it was absolutely delicious. He felt that he had never tasted such fine food in the palace when *he* was king. He supped it up quickly, and almost forgot his manners. Then came the main course: it was steak and mushroom pie, with buttered asparagus on the side. A servant asked: 'Some red wine, sir?' Boris was in ecstasy. He remembered the label on the bottle as the servant filled his glass. He sipped and thought: 'I must have had this wine before, but it never tasted as good as this. The wine and the food – it seemed that he had never tasted anything like it before. Then came the dessert – rhubarb crumble with real custard. 'Oh, my favourite,' Boris groaned in satisfaction.

When the lunch was over they needed time to relax. King Albert invited Boris to the royal library for coffee. Halfway through his first cup, Boris had come to his senses, and he remembered his clever plan. 'Now let's get down to business,' Boris said. 'The country is in a mess and we need to do something about it.'

'I agree,' said King Albert. 'That is why I invited you here today. Have you anything to suggest?'

'Yes,' said Boris. 'You want to stick to *The Book of Laws,* don't you?'

'Er … Yes,' said Albert, with slight hesitation, not knowing where this would lead.

Boris continued: 'You became … er … king at eight o'clock on the morning on the first day of this month.' Albert nodded, just a little, to be polite.

'So today you are in the first year of your reign.'

'Yes, definitely,' said Albert.

Boris then revealed his master-stroke: 'Well, just a tiniest fraction of a second after eight o'clock in the morning on the first day of April next, you will enter the *second* year of your reign!' He did not give Albert much time to react.

Boris continued: 'So it will *then* be an *even*-numbered year in your reign. I will make sure by the previous day that I am clearly the poorest peasant, and then you and I will have to swap places, according to *The Book of Laws*.'

Boris glared at Albert: 'And if you give up now I shall pardon you for your impudence.' Smiling smugly, he sat back in his chair, and waited for Albert's reaction. 'It was checkmate,' he thought to himself. 'The fake king is cornered.'

Boris knew that Albert had put an Article in *The Book of Laws* saying that Boris could not be king again. But Boris's plan was to change his name slightly – to Boriss – if he gained power, to get round this law. But first he needed to regain power as king, when he would declare his slight change of name.

Albert knew that Boris knew that *The Book of Laws* now said that Boris could not be king again, and Albert guessed that Boris might have some plan to deal with this. The important thing was to make sure that Boris never ever became king, even for a few hours. If he regained power he could change the rules, as Albert had done. So Albert carefully responded to Boris.

'But you remember,' said Albert, 'there was a slight delay this year? You had to send someone to go back into the palace and find your spectacles. The ceremony did not start until about ten minutes after eight o'clock. And I did not become king for the day until several minutes had passed after that.'

Boris responded: '… er, yes',

Albert continued: 'Next year I shall make sure that we start precisely on time. By the time that I have finished my announcement and everyone is put in their new positions, no more than ten minutes will have passed and I shall still be in the first year of my reign. It will thus be still an odd-numbered year. We shall simply swap places for the day with our wives and have the usual fun. But you and your wife will remain in your farmhouse, according to the *Book of Laws*.'

Boris was outwitted. He thought desperately for a while, and then spoke again: 'OK, but what about the year after next. You and I are bound to change places then! It must *then* be an even-numbered year. I've got less than two years to wait and I'll be king once more.'

'No,' said Albert. 'I shall find an excuse – like finding my spectacles – to delay the ceremony by ten minutes or more. People are used to bumbling delays, especially with kings. I shall then have been king for a little bit more than two years. I will have entered the third year of my reign. It will then be an odd-numbered year. We shall simply swap places with our wives again.'

Albert paused, leaned toward Boris and looked him in the eye: 'I shall arrange things so that we always change places when I have reigned for an odd number of years. Every year, people will change places just after eight o'clock, or just after ten minutes past eight o'clock, so when that happens my reign is always in an odd-numbered year. When we change places on April Fools' Days, it will *never ever* be an even-numbered year again, at least as long as I rule. People will eventually forget what happens on the first day in April on even-numbered years. Anyway they enjoy themselves much more on odd-numbered years. They will prefer the new arrangement. Give up Boris: you will never be king again. You are older than I, you are fat and unfit, and you will most probably die before me. I am your king for the rest of your life. Get used to it.'

At that point King Albert ended the meeting: 'Thank you so much for visiting me today. It was very kind of you, especially with all the things you need to attend to on the farm. I have much enjoyed our discussion. But we still have not sorted out all the problems in the country, so would you kindly accept my invitation to come round here for another modest lunch again tomorrow?'

Boris nodded, and muttered some words of thanks. Once again, he almost forgot his manners.

Walking back to the farm, Boris reflected. He blamed his Prime Minister for placing someone so clever at the lowest rank on the first day of April that year. 'How could that bumbling idiot of a Prime Minister get it so wrong' he thought to himself. 'If I ever become king again I'll remove him from his job.'

But then he realised that the former Prime Minister had already been removed from his job and he was now a peasant farmer. At least Boris could gain a tiny bit of satisfaction from the current state of affairs.

With that small, sweet morsel of satisfaction, Boris entered the bed in the farmhouse and fell asleep. But he was not entirely happy and he would have to meet King Albert again.

10. King Albert and Boris Meet at the Palace Again

Boris was looking forward to lunch again when he walked up to the palace the next day. He reached the front door and was invited into the palace. A few minutes later lunch was served. Sure enough, it was a lovely meal. This time they started with a delicious mushroom soup, with just the right amount of herbs for added flavour. This was followed by a very tasty vegetarian lasagne with lentils, and then a most delightful apple tart with just a hint of cinnamon and nutmeg, served with thick, delicious cream.

'Thank you King Albert,' Boris said, 'for such a tasty meal.'

'My pleasure,' said Albert, 'but let's go to the library for coffee, and get down to business. This time *I* have a suggestion to make.'

They sat down in the library and coffee was served. King Albert thanked the servants: 'Thank you. But that will be all for now. I do not wish to be disturbed for the next hour.'

Albert turned to Boris: 'Boris my friend, allow me to suggest that you don't *really* want to be king. Not *really*.'

At first Boris tried to interrupt and deny this, but Albert stopped him and said: 'Allow me to continue, you can have your say when I have finished.'

Albert explained: 'I think I know you better. You love gambling and playing cards. But you hate all the nobles and their pomposity. What you really want is to be comfortable and have enough money to spend to enjoy yourself. In truth you would like some real friends, who were not stuffed-up lords or ladies, who enjoyed playing cards and gambling and spending their money on good food and wine. You want some friends who like you for what you really are, rather than sucking up to you for favours just because you are king.'

'Think about it Boris, that is what you *really* want, isn't it? It might seem odd to others who are not in the know like us, but being king gives you little freedom. You always have to dress up properly and be nice to people. You have to *pretend* to like people that you *really* dislike. You have many tedious ceremonies to attend. You can rarely do what you really want. A king is unfree. A king can never let himself go. A king has to play an official role, rather than being himself. You don't *really* want to be King Boris, do you?'

Boris thought for a while and he knew that Albert was right. Albert had finished speaking, so Boris said: 'But I never had the chance. I became king because my father had been king before. I had responsibilities. It was not proper for me to mix with any of the lower orders. Instead I had to mix with all those stuffy and boring lords and ladies. Now it is even worse. I am one of the poorest peasants. No-one wants to go out with me for a bit of fun, and I can't afford a night on the town anyway.'

Albert said: 'So I am right, aren't I? You do not really want to be a king.' Boris looked very sorry for himself and admitted: 'Yes, I suppose.'

'What if I were to give you *everything* you *really* want?' asked Albert.

'But how?' was the response. 'How is that possible?'

Albert explained: 'You know the kingdom much better than I. After all, you were king for much longer. I could not afford to travel before I became king. I've not been there yet, but people say that much further down the river, where it gets wider and just before it meets the sea, there is a village. What is its name?'

'That's the village of Lowdown,' said Boris.

'Well I want you to be the Mayor of Lowdown, said Albert, and I want you to turn it into a big, bustling prosperous town. I will give you two thousand silver crowns from my treasury. You can then invest the money on gambling casinos and music halls and theatres and everything else you enjoy.'

'Sounds great,' said Boris, getting a little excited. 'I know, I could turn it into a port to trade with other countries and import some really excellent food and wine.' 'Fantastic idea!' said Albert.

Boris got even more excited: 'There would be so much money to make in this town, and so much fun to be had in the theatres and casinos, that it would become prosperous. Everyone would want to come to live there. And then even more money would be made. Many people would come to visit from other countries, and everyone in Lowdown would make even more money …'

Albert nodded. Boris continued: 'And because there would be so much money and so many markets, people could then even bet on whether prices would go up or down, and have even more fun.'

'Now you are getting carried away with yourself,' said Albert. 'But I see you like the idea. Are you up for it?'

'Yes,' said Boris. 'But I'll do it for no less than three thousand crowns.'

'Deal!' said Albert. 'I agree. But there is a hitch.'

'What?' was the perplexed response. 'It's a great idea and we've done a deal, haven't we?'

Albert explained: 'The hitch is *The Book of Laws*. The book was fine when everything was in order and nothing changed. But things will change and one day in the future some of the rules will have to go.'

'Consider this: when I die there will be a new king and eventually there will be an even-numbered year. Then on the first of April on an even-numbered year they will have to give everyone a rank. But by then, at least in Lowdown, there will be new jobs, such as gambling casino manager, and theatre owner, and professional actress. None of these are listed in the book. Who would change places with whom? It would be chaos.'

'So what must be done?' asked Boris.

Albert had worked this out already. 'We'll keep to *The Book of Laws* as much as possible, but hide it away. At first we'll have to add lots of new laws. Eventually one of the new laws will contradict one of the old laws written in the book. And for the king that follows me, we shall have to abolish the even-numbered April Fools' Day law, well before I die. For these reasons, we have to keep the book secret, especially because it is written in it that no law can ever be changed. As it stands, *The Book of Laws* is too difficult to change. I really do not see any other way out of the problem, especially if this country is going to improve.'

Boris did not seem to be that bothered by the idea. In fact he tried to help: 'You could hire lawyers, who write down all the new laws in a complicated language that few people can understand. And these lawyers can then make money by being hired to argue which lawyer is right or wrong in their interpretation of the law,' laughed Boris. 'I can have lots of these lawyers in Lowdown.'

Albert continued with his argument: 'But if we keep *The Book of Laws* secret, then it could not help stop a revolt, like it did two days ago. It could not be used to endorse the positions of the lords or the king. It would have to remain out of sight. I've thought long and hard about this, but I do not see any other way. *The Book of Laws* must be kept hidden.'

'Why?' asked Boris.

'If the book of laws was brought out to show everyone's proper place, then they might inspect the book and find that we had put in new laws that overturned old ones. The book would have laws that contradicted one another. Then no-one would respect *The Book of Laws* anymore.'

'So how would be the positions of the noble and royal families be upheld?' asked Boris. 'How would we know who was a rightful ruler, or rightful lord, or rightful lady, or rightful landlord? How would we be able to tell?'

'Unfortunately, in the end,' Albert replied, 'might would become right. These kinds of decisions would be made by force of arms. If a king were challenged, it might come to a battle, and the winner of the battle would be declared and assumed as the rightful king.'

'But what if, in truth, he had no right to be king?' asked Boris.

'Then tough on everyone, including those that tried to challenge his rule. With great regret, force would be the ultimate ruler. Once we start contradicting *The Book of Laws* then we have no alternative. So far I have not broken any laws in *The Book of Laws,* but when I stayed in power after eight o'clock in the evening on the first of April, I overturned tradition and the unwritten law.'

'So what should be done?' asked Boris.

'I plan to train a loyal army, to protect me, my family and our royal descendants from usurpers. I'm going to start on that tomorrow.'

'What else are you going to do?'

'The other things I want to do will require your agreement.'

'My agreement?' Boris asked.

Albert continued: 'Yes, you must swear not to tell anyone what we have discussed today, and you must also agree that from now *The Book of Laws* is to be kept secret. If anyone asks you must not give away too many details about its contents. Just say that everything is in order, to re-assure people. If they ever thought they were ruled by people who gained their status by force, then they would become upset or angry. If everything goes according to plan, then I shall give you the three thousand silver crowns before the end of next month.'

'I swear, and agree,' said Boris. 'So what are you going to do next?'

Albert answered: 'I am also going to make a new law tomorrow that allows any two families, if they both agree voluntarily and without coercion, to swap places without having to return to their former positions. So if one of those new peasants wants to swap with a former peasant, then that will be allowed under the new law. It would be very helpful you could help me by pretending that this is all in accord with *The Book of Laws,* while secretly we both know that it is not.'

'Fine with me,' said Boris. And strangely, after all this time, they both began to feel they were almost friends.

'What about husbands changing places with their wives?' asked Boris with a smile.

'Well they can now do that on *every* April Fools' Day!' said Albert chuckling. 'Can I come and visit you in Lowdown when you are all set up?'

'Definitely,' said Boris. 'Once things are up and running you can come and visit Lowdown any time. You will be made very welcome. It will be good for the tourists to have you there. Come to think of it, I'll even build you another royal palace, near the centre of town. That will do wonders for the tourist trade.'

'That would be great,' said Albert, 'I'd love to come to Lowdown often'. They shook hands warmly and parted for the day. Both of them were happy with the deal. Boris especially looked forward to his new life as Mayor of Lowdown. They both slept very soundly that night.

11. King Albert Makes More Laws

It all happened according to plan. The next day King Albert announced his new law allowing families voluntarily to swap places. In a few days this new law was so popular that no-one bothered to ask whether it was according to *The Book of Laws* or not. People who really wanted to farm the land became farmers. Those who did not like farming, or were no good at it, swapped with someone who did.

Families who were bored with being lords, ladies or a landowners, or found their large houses too draughty or difficult to clean, swapped with others who thought that social status was everything and did not want a small house or a more active job.

As far as possible, people picked the jobs they were good at, or that they enjoyed most and this helped to increase productivity throughout the economy. Bit by bit, everyone became happier.

Soon more food was being produced and the markets re-opened. As more and more food came in, prices fell. By the end of May no-one was starving any more, and the people as a whole were much happier.

Albert recruited an army, and paid them all well. They all took an oath of loyalty to their king and country, but not to *The Book of Laws*. No-one noticed the omission. The soldiers looked very fine in their new smart uniforms, and they were very proud of their job protecting the king, who was becoming more and more popular every day.

In June, Boris and his family moved to Lowdown. Boris gave a bit of his money to Blossom and she opened a beauty salon. He gave the same amount of money to Bruce, and he opened a pub. Eventually Boris developed Lowdown into a thriving port, and its inhabitants got richer and richer. There were hotels, and markets and casinos and much else. The merchants sometimes argued between themselves over their business deals, so there was lots of work for lawyers to sort things out.

By the fifth year of his reign Albert was the most popular king that had ever ruled the small country. He was always cheered loudly when he mixed with the people. No-one opposed him, or tried to take away his power. But he kept his small army fit and ready, just in case.

Albert decided that it was about time that his country had a name. After all, it was receiving more and more visitors, and many tourists were coming, especially to Lowdown. Its population was increasing rapidly and it was becoming more prosperous and well-known. But there was no name to put on the tourist brochures. A country without a name just wasn't good for business.

Albert wanted something short, snappy and easy to remember. He thought about this problem for several days. Then his mind turned to *The Book of Laws of the Land of* ▄▄▄ .

'I've got it!' he said to himself. 'It will be called Inkland!'

Albert announced this formally to the people at a great ceremony, where he made a speech to a large crowd: 'Welcome, good people. We are now a great and prosperous country. ...'

'Long live King Albert!' someone shouted from the crowd. This led to a great cheer.

'Thank you, kind people,' Albert responded. 'Because of our greatness and our prosperity, it is about time that our country had a name.' There was another huge cheer.

'From henceforth I declare that this country will be called the Kingdom of Inkland!' There was another loud cheer from the crowd. The trumpets sounded. The king mounted his horse, and to still more cheers he rode down the street, followed by his soldiers, who all marched perfectly together, in line and in step.

The people liked the new name for their country and it stuck. They called themselves Inklanders.

Albert was a great and very wise king. He was far below average height, and not very handsome. Yet he was adored by his people. They admired him for his wisdom and for creating a sense of national pride; and everyone was so much better off than before.

In the tenth year of his reign, Princess Annie was old enough to marry. Although she was short, she was taller than her parents. She was intelligent and quite pretty, and she already had a boyfriend called Archibald. He was much taller than her, good fun and quite handsome. With King Albert's warm approval they decided to get married.

There was a great royal wedding with lots of ceremony. It took place in Lowdown, which by now was by far the largest town in the land. Boris had kept his promise to build in Lowdown a second palace for Albert and the royal family. A year later the newly-wed royal couple had a son called Arthur. Prince Arthur grew up to be quite tall and quite handsome. He was declared officially as King Albert's heir.

Albert had discussed with Annie whether she wanted to be queen after he died. But Annie decided against the idea. She decided instead to become a scientist and help her son Arthur when new ideas and inventions when he became king. She collected a great number of books and held classes with many students. She became renowned for her wisdom and learning.

As Albert had predicted, Boris died before him. But Boris had had a fulfilling time as Mayor of Lowdown. He did things that he enjoyed doing. In this new job he had been much happier than when he was king. Also Albert and Boris had become good friends. Eventually, over the centuries, some of Boris's descendants also became mayors of that town.

Eventually, after many more years had passed, Albert was taken ill and he was confined by his doctors to his bed. The people got very worried and sent him messages hoping that he would get better. They would refer to him far and wide as 'King Albert the Great.' A few weeks later, despite the best efforts of his doctors, Albert passed away peacefully in his bed.

'The King is dead! Long live the king!' By the latter, of course, they referred to the new king, King Arthur. But the people were beyond themselves with sadness and they mourned for a whole month. King Albert's funeral in Lowdown was a huge and very sad affair, with hundreds of people attending.

Although he was physically small and could not fight well in battles, Inkland had had its greatest and wisest ruler ever. Under the clever leadership of King Albert, the country had become happier and wealthier. It would be a long time before times were as good as that again.

So let us reflect for a moment on the reign of King Albert the Great and the good things that he did. In particular, we should never make the serious mistake of assuming that only rich, tall or handsome people are clever. But if the Prime Minister had not made that mistake, then Albert would never have become king.

But what happened to *The Book of Laws* after King Albert died? That is the subject of the next and final chapter.

12. Where is *The Book of Laws?*

King Arthur was the grandson of King Albert the Great. For a few years Arthur's reign was peaceful. But he got irritated by some of his lords, so he bought them some metal helmets and chain mail, and called them knights. Instead of just hanging around the palace looking bored and waiting for royal favours, Arthur asked that they try jousting, killing dragons or rescuing damsels in distress.

But that didn't work. The knights couldn't find any dragons anywhere, jousting was expensive and a bit dangerous, and there weren't many damsels in distress. So Arthur bought them a very large round table from a local carpenter. 'This is my gift to you. Why don't you gamble and play cards on it?' he suggested.

But that didn't work either, and the knights got even more annoying. He even suspected that one of them was messing about with his wife. So King Arthur sent them all off on a long quest to find some old cup, and made up a story about it being very special.

But eventually he had to call them back, because there was disorder in Inkland. Arthur and his knights had to fight several battles against angry people (called Sacksons) who were so poor that they wore brown sacks for uniforms. The Sacksons wanted Inkland for themselves, but they were eventually defeated in a big battle. There was peace for a while, but the Sacksons attacked again and this time King Arthur was tragically killed in another great battle.

Inkland was already in the Dark Ages, but then it got even darker. It got so dark that documents were hard to read or write. Many of them got lost in the dark. So there was a succession of wars and kings, but we don't know much about them. But we do know that for a long time Inkland was divided into several kingdoms, which were always arguing and fighting with each other.

Because of the Dark Ages, people could not see very much when they tried swapping clothes on the first day of April each year. Being unable to laugh at each other because of the dark, less fun was to be had and so this tradition died out.

Then the Dark Ages began to end, and it got a bit brighter. By then all the people could then remember was that April the first was a day when we they had fun, and played jokes on each other, and said: 'April Fool!' They had forgotten about changing clothes.

When it became a great deal brighter, people began to write things down again. But their spelling had got worse and they had lost many old documents in the Dark Ages. They began to call the country England instead of Inkland, Sacksons became Saxons and Lowdown became London. These were clearly spelling errors, but many people made mistakes with their spelling in the Dark Ages, for obvious and understandable reasons.

Although it was just a spelling error, 'England' sounded a much more attractive place to conquer than 'Inkland'. So this particular spelling error caused a lot of trouble. Foreign kings wanted to conquer England. Eventually England was successfully invaded by a William from France who killed England's King Harold in a famous battle. This William was very brutal, and he was not very good when it came to marketing. The only name he could think of for himself was 'William the Conqueror.' This wasn't very inventive, and there was no need to rub it in.

Every time a new king came to rule Inkland – or England as it was now called – they would make sure that *The Book of Laws* was safely hidden away and out of reach. If that book ever came to light, then there would be big trouble.

This went on for centuries until the reign of King Charles the First. He annoyed so many people that they had his head chopped off. They tried having no king at all, but that didn't work either. Those who were left in charge did some good things but they completely ignored *The Book of Laws*. They tried making some new laws. They argued and argued, and eventually decided to abolish Christmas. This was even more upsetting. Someone wrote a song about the end of the old laws and traditions, called 'The World Turned Upside Down.'

Because the experiment making new laws without a king failed, the nobles and other leaders brought over from France the son of the executed king. He too was called Charles. He became the King of England and also kept *The Book of Laws* locked safely away.

King Charles the Second was married to Queen Catherine. But he fell in love with a beautiful orange-seller called Nell Gwyn. Then he died, and his son James took over as king. But many people did not like James, and William from Holland invaded England. He too liked oranges. Because of that he was called William of Orange.

After that, England had had enough of being invaded, so its leaders decided that they were going to invade other places instead. One of many places they had already invaded was America. Almost a hundred years after the invasion of William of Orange, King George the Third was on the throne. He ruled America as well as England.

King George and the English Parliament had imposed a large tax on the tea imported into America. This made some Americans very angry (or mad as the Americans say). So they threw the expensive tea into the sea, which was a bit of a waste of good tea.

One American had heard about *The Book of Laws,* so he suggested that they should go to the royal palace in London and ask to see it. So a group of Americans came over to London pretending to be tourists. They thought that this large tax might not be supported by *The Book of Laws.* If they could see the book, then they could find out if the tax was legal or illegal. If it were not in *The Book of Laws,* then they could appeal to the king for the tax to be stopped. Americans can be a bit brash and bold, so they sometimes do things like that.

But when they got to the palace, the king refused to let them see the book. The Americans argued, demanding the right to see *The Book of Laws,* which was supposed to contain all the rules and regulations that affected their lives. The Americans eventually declared that if they were not allowed to see it, then they would go back home across the Atlantic and write down their very own book of laws. 'So stick that in your rule book, buddy!' one said rudely as they turned around and left the king.

The American visitors returned to their homes and reported to other leading Americans this conversation with the king. These top Americans told King George that they would now run their own country. And they would start writing down their own book of laws. They would call it a *Constitution*, so that it would not be confused with the English *Book of Laws*. Hearing of all this, King George got so angry (or mad as the Americans say) that he sent over an army to America. But there he was defeated by another leader called George, and King George of England had to give up his American colony and allow this other George to rule America as its first President. This made King George of England a bit mad (or crazy as the Americans like to say).

When the British Army in America surrendered to the Americans, they played the tune of the old song 'The World Turned Upside Down'. This was to remind the Americans that unless they were very careful, then they too could mess things up when they were in charge. In fact, they messed things up several times.

Because they made so many mistakes in their writing, and they could not easily agree on the details, it took them several years to agree upon their *Constitution*. Even then, they had to copy many English laws. After that they quickly realised that the first draft was not good enough, and so they had to keep adding amendments.

Since their independence, Americans have got much worse at spelling and they get the meanings of some words mixed up. For example, they write 'labor' instead of 'labour'. They confuse 'angry' with 'mad' and call 'lifts' 'elevators'. They describe 'biscuits' as 'cookies' and call the autumn 'fall'. But when you meet an American you must keep all this to yourself and be very polite. They don't like to be reminded that they made many mistakes after they were allowed to rule themselves.

Today London is especially rich, but we are not sure if its people are as happy. Many people in London spend money gambling on whether prices will go up or down – as Mayor Boris predicted long ago – but sometimes they lose lots of money and they all get very upset. Then they have the cheek to go to the government and ask for more money. Once a Prime Minister felt sorry for them for losing so much money through gambling. So he helped them with huge payments from the public treasury. But then the Prime Minister had to put up taxes to get the money back, which made even more people upset, especially as most the taxes went on people who did not gamble away the money in the first place.

There have been many new laws since the time of King Albert the Great. But they still kept some of the very old laws from *The Book of Laws,* including the one that says that people who commit treason by trying to overthrow the king or queen will be hanged. That was still the law of England until 1998.

The king and queen have soldiers to protect them from those who want to seize the throne by force. But we now elect the people who choose Prime Ministers, so sometimes we can vote to get rid of those that do not do their job very well. Because they are elected, and because there are so many new laws made every year, Prime Ministers now work a great deal harder than in King Albert's time, even if they sometimes make big mistakes. It took a very long time to decide to give every adult the vote. And we still do not vote on who is going to be king or queen. But some people say that it is for the best.

Few people know about the secret and hidden side of English history that has been told in this book, including the real reason why America became independent. But now you know the truth about English history.

Even fewer people know that *The Book of Laws* is still hidden in a secret vault in one of the royal palaces. Some university professors try and cover this all up by repeating endlessly that 'England has *not* got a written constitution'. They are trying to pull the wool over our eyes. But England really has all its oldest laws written down in one place. It's called *The Book of Laws*. It is hidden away somewhere, probably in a royal palace or a royal castle.

If the truth ever came to light, then there would be a huge fuss. We would all discover that English society has long been turned upside down, ever since King Albert came to throne on that April Fools' Day, many hundreds of years ago. Although he was a tiny person, he turned his world upside down, and it has remained so ever since. Will anyone *ever* put it the right way up again? Or would it be safer to leave things just as they are? What do *you* think?